# HOW TO HAVE A BIRTHDAY

Mary Lyn Ray

*illustrated by* Cindy Derby

Candlewick Press

On the morning of your birthday,

you can tell already that the day is not like others.

Maybe you wake early, wondering what will happen.

You know *something* will.

And that's your first present: you get to wonder.

There may be whispered plans.
There may be—

who knows yet?

At breakfast you might be given a crown.

Because your birthday is to celebrate that you are here.
It's to tell you that you matter.

People may sing to you.

Or you can make up a little song and sing it to yourself.

You don't have to wait for someone else.

A birthday is the first day, too, you can try out
how it's different being one year older.

*And?* On your birthday there will probably
be a present wrapped in special paper.

Or there may be lots—

though sometimes the best one is knowing the whole day is yours.

Because wherever you go,
your birthday goes with you.

To remember the day, it's good to have pictures—
even if it means remembering that haircut you'd
rather forget or when you had to wear what you
said you *wouldn't, wouldn't, wouldn't.*

If every year you do something the same
on your birthday, then you have A Tradition.

Or every year you might do something new.
That can also be a tradition.

Or you might just wait to be surprised.

Because something always happens, anyway,
to remind you what the day is.

And then you feel again that shivery feeling
that belongs only to a birthday.

The one rule for birthdays is that everybody
gets one—*though just one*—every year.

There's also this: *birthday cake.*

So don't forget to practice blowing.
Because all year you're growing toward another candle.

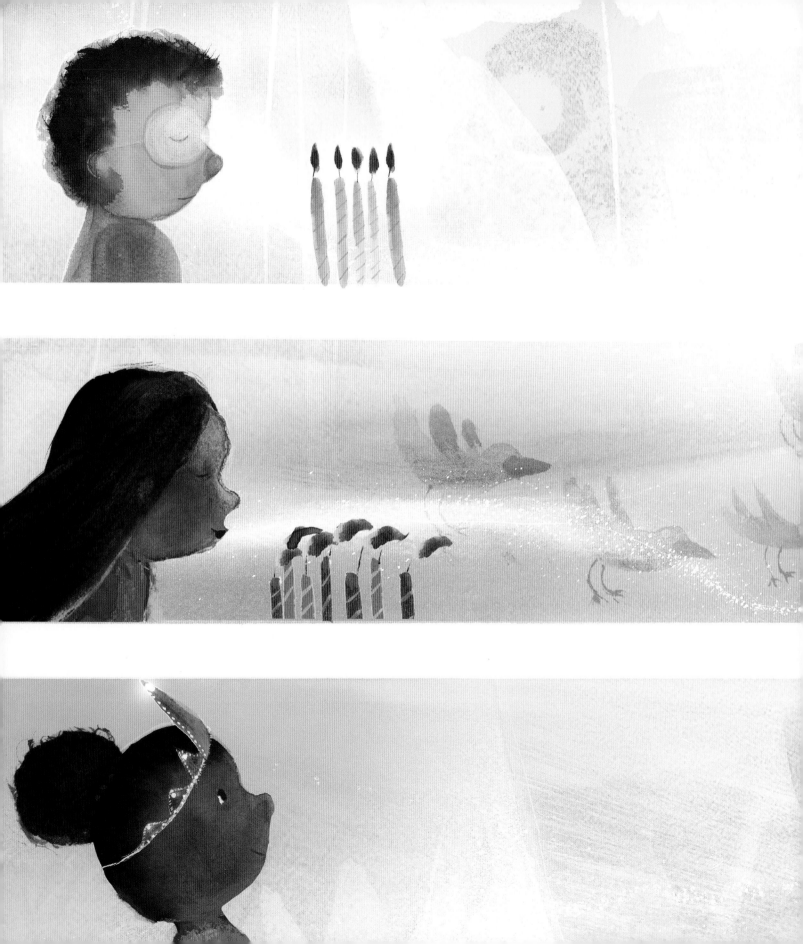

And then it's time to close your eyes and wish.

All year you can think about your wish.
But on your birthday, you get to make it.

(After that, you have to wait and see.)

Almost anything could happen.

But what's for sure is that
your birthday is all yours to unwrap.

For everyone who has a birthday
MLR

For Jeremy & Sam
CD

First edition 2021

Library of Congress Catalog Card Number pending
ISBN 978-1-5362-0741-5

21 22 23 24 25 26 CCP 10 9 8 7 6 5 4 3 2 1

Printed in Shenzhen, Guangdong, China

This book was typeset in Alegreya.
The illustrations were created on the road in a camper van with watercolor,
pastels, coloring pencils, gouache, and a few sprinkles.

Candlewick Press
99 Dover Street
Somerville, Massachusetts 02144

www.candlewick.com